SYLVESTER THE JESTER

A BOOK ABOUT ACCEPTING OTHERS

Michael P. Waite
Illustrated by Anthony DeRosa

Chariot Books™
David C. Cook Publishing Co.

For Karen Hesse and all my pals at the Newfane Writer's Group. MPW

To Janie Marie, daddy's little girl. AJD

Chariot Books™ is an imprint of David C. Cook Publishing Co.
David C. Cook Publishing Co., Elgin, Illinois 60120
David C. Cook Publishing Co., Weston, Ontario
Nova Distribution Ltd., Newton Abbot, England

SYLVESTER THE JESTER
© 1992 by Michael P. Waite for text and illustrations

Designed by Studio North
First Printing, 1992
Printed in the United States of America
96 95 94 93   5 4 3

Library of Congress Cataloging-in-Publication Data
Waite, Michael P., 1960-
    Sylvester the jester / Michael P. Waite; illustrated by Anthony DeRosa.
    p. cm. — (Building Christian character)
    Summary: Sylvester the Jester bars the Orange-Spotted Bingles from the Royal Feast because they look different.
    ISBN 0-7814-0033-3
    [1. Prejudices—Fiction. 2. Middle Ages—Fiction. 3. Stories in rhyme.]
I. DeRosa, Anthony, ill. II. Title. III. Series: Waite, Michael P., 1960- Building Christian character.
PZ8.3.W136Sy 1992   91-38875
[E]—dc20   CIP   AC

You've heard the tales from days of old
Of famous queens and kings,
Of castles grand and questing knights
And other wondrous things.
But have you heard the splendid tale
Of jolly old Sylvester?
He lived in Bingland long ago—
The kingdom's finest jester.

Sylvester served the King and Queen,
He served them smiles and laughter!
He juggled jugs
And mugs and rugs
(And bowed politely after).

He danced on stilts and played the flute.
(O how he made the poor thing toot!)
He wore a jingly-tingly suit
And dangled from a rafter.

His greatest show came once a month,
When every man and beast
Would gather on the castle lawn
To join the Royal Feast.

O what a day of food and song!
The knights played daring games—
Sylvester made the rules, of course,
And gave them silly names:

A jousting match called Tickle-Toss
(You need a ten-foot feather!)

And Target-Topple-Archery
(To win, you must be clever!)

8

Then when at last the games were through,
They gathered round the moat,
And SPLASH! they hopped in all at once
To slosh and wash and float!

9

This is how the Royal Feast
Was run by dear Sylvester,
Until one day, he watched the crowd
And something struck the jester:

"Oh dear!" he told the King and Queen,
"There's something awfully wrong—
Those orange-spotted Bingles! See?
They're strange. They don't belong."
The King and Queen stood up and stared,
And instantly they both declared,
"My boy, you're RIGHT! We must be spared!
Please have them move along!"

And after that, a sign went up
Outside the castle wall:
NO ORANGE-SPOTTED BINGLES PLEASE!!!
It said—
And that was all.

The Royal Feast soon came again;
Sylvester watched the crowd,
And spying something very odd,
He spoke his mind out loud:
"O dearest Queen, O grandest King,
I notice now an awful thing!
Those Bingles there, with hair like string—
With curly-cues that sprout and spring—
They're odd as owls without a wing!
They ought not be allowed!"

12

The King and Queen forthright agreed
And so the castle sign decreed:
NO ORANGE-SPOTTED BINGLES PLEASE!!!
NO CURLY-HEADED BINGLES PLEASE!!!
For everyone to read.

Sylvester now surveyed his Feast,
His puffed-up pride was double.
But when the King and Queen looked down,
He knew he was in trouble.

"Sylvester!" called the crooning King,
"I fear I have bad tidings!
The Queen and I are quite displeased
By all of these abidings,
For there are Bingles in this crowd,
With stout and skinny features!
And naturally, we can't allow
Such odd, unhealthy creatures!"

Sylvester gazed upon his belt—
His knees felt just like jelly!
Because he knew that he was stout,
Especially 'round the belly!

So now Sylvester stood outside
And read the castle sign:
NO ORANGE-SPOTTED BINGLES PLEASE!!!
NO CURLY-HEADED BINGLES PLEASE!!!
NO STOUT OR SKINNY BINGLES PLEASE!!!
Then he shuffled down the hill
And left his home behind.

A month had passed, or maybe two,
Since he'd left the castle.
Sylvester sat and moped and moaned,
Tugging on a tassel.

Then out of nowhere, through the sky
There roared a streak of fire—
A dragon spouting streams of smoke!
It growled and glided higher.

"It's heading for the castle walls!"
Sylvester gasped in fear—
"The King and Queen will both be trapped!
What shall I do? Oh dear!"

"It serves them right!" snapped Sir Duaine,
For he was orange-spotted.
"Who needs their kind?" said Lady Lydd,
And all the others nodded.

The sky was now as black as soot,
The castle lost in smoke,
Sylvester struggled through the crowd
And angrily he spoke:

"Listen, please! For I'm to blame!
'Twas I who told the King
That orange-spots and curly hair
Were not a normal thing.
I'm sorry for this sad mistake—
For I was very wrong;
It isn't spots or skin or hair,
But hearts that make us strong!

"Now here's our chance to show the King
Just what we have inside
And that a Bingle can't be judged
By belly, hair, or hide!
Now gather 'round, I have a plan,
I think you'll find it keen!
Together we can prove ourselves,
And save the King and Queen!"

The dragon held the King and Queen
Inside the banquet hall.
He made them clean the cupboards bare
While he devoured it all!

He roasted rugs and chairs and stairs
And piles of precious things,
And now his fearsome fiery eyes
Were glaring at the King!

Through the door Sylvester charged,
The archers at his side!
The dragon roared around to fight,
And arrows hailed his hide.

Suction-cups clamped up his mouth
And blinded both his eyes.
He writhed and rumbled 'round the room
Scratching at the skies.

25

Now the jousting knights appeared,
Their feathers at the ready.
The dragon swung his scaly tail,
But all the knights held steady.

They bore down on his ticklish toes,
Their skill so very clever,
The dragon reeled away so fast
He did not feel the window blast
The castle walls went rumbling past
Till SPLASH! he struck the moat at last
And quenched his fire forever!

The King and Queen were overjoyed!
They hugged and kissed Sylvester.
"O please forgive us!" they implored,
"Come back and be our jester!"

From that day on, the King and Queen
Made all the Bingles proud
By putting up a sign that said:
BINGLES ALL ALLOWED!!!

And at the Royal Feast you'd see
Everyone in Bingdom—
For everybody plays a part
In making up the kingdom!